Ankaa

Allwyn Rise

Published by Eureka Tales, 2023.

Also by Allwyn Rise

Ankaa

Table of Contents

Ankaa
Allwyn Rise

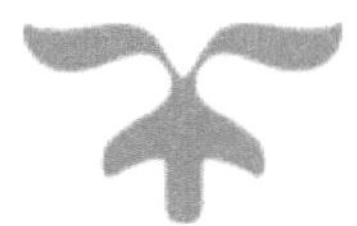

COPYRIGHT PAGE

Title: Ankaa

Author: Allwyn Rise

Editor: M Safee

Extended English Manuscript: A.I

Translator: A.I

Book Cover Illustration: Canva A.I generated

Registered Business Name: EurekaTales Enterprise

Proof-reader: M Safee

Published by: EurekaTales

Chapter 1: The Considerate King

"Dear heaven,
Let my hope resound,
In a world seemingly deaf,
May miracles bloom one day,
Under the warmth of the sun,
I'll hold sunflowers in my hands,
Rising above the depths of the sea."

IN A KINGDOM FAVORED with harmony and flourishing, there ruled a shrewd and big-hearted King known for his benevolence and empathy. His name was King Aryan, and he controlled with a delicate hand, continuously looking seeking the welfare of his subjects. Other than being an equitable King, he was a doting dad to two kids - a son named Prince Joshua and a daughter named Princess Chenoa.

Prince Joshua was the exemplification of effortlessness and appeal, appreciated by all who put complete focus on him. With his enthralling grin and honorable disposition, he had won the hearts of individuals. Princess Chenoa, then again, was a dream of magnificence and pleasantness. Her charming atmosphere and warm character charmed her to everybody she experienced.

The royal kins were indistinguishable and were consistently by their dad's side, offering support and direction in the issues of the kingdom.

Their presence gave pleasure and satisfaction to the King, who found comfort in their organization during moments of bliss and misery.

As the sun plunged beneath the skyline, flagging the finish of one more prosperous day in the kingdom, the imperial family would frequently accumulate in the stupendous corridor of the royal residence. There, they would talk about issues of the state, share stories, and relax in the glow of their bond.

Nonetheless, unbeknownst to individuals of the kingdom, there was a mystery that King Aryan monitored intently. A dull and puzzling condemnation had happened to his dearest girl, Princess Chenoa. As night dropped upon the kingdom, she would change into a fearsome mythical beast, her delicate nature supplanted by a threatening presence. A dragon.

Every evening, as the sun plunged beneath the skyline, the King would lead his girl to a stupendous and detached chamber concealed inside the castle. There, Princess Chenoa would be safely bound and avoided the world, guaranteeing that she could not hurt anyone during her mythical scaled-monstrous form.

The moon's gentle glow bathed the dark forest in a silver radiance, and Princess Chenoa looked at the moon from the window and stood beneath its luminous embrace. With a heavy heart, she gazed at the celestial orb and whispered, "Dear Moon, you look so beautiful, radiant, and pure. Yet here I am, a wretched creature, cursed to this draconian form. I'm so scared, dear moon, but I hope your light can somehow dispel the darkness that engulfs me."

The curse had been severely put on her by an evil wicked witch whom had a longed intention to unleash destruction on the noble family. King Aryan had maintained this mystery stowed away from the world, expecting that the disclosure would bring confusion and depression. To safeguard his girl and the kingdom's tranquility, he formulated an arrangement to keep her concealed during her repulsive change.

In spite of the weight of this secrecy, King Aryan and his kids remained the strengths for each other. Together, they confronted the difficulties of governing the kingdom and the burden of a hidden curse, joined in their affection and backing for each other. Much to their dismay that destiny had bound them for an unparalleled journey loaded up with trials, boldness, and the genuine substance of a kind heart.

"Don't worry, my beloved daughter; I will be here for you. May your worries be gone someday. I will protect you until my last breath." He whispered as he was holding his chest with his hand while looking at his daughter through the secret window, who was sleeping as a dragon creature.

Chapter 2: The Brave Princess

"I'm on my own now,
I don't want to be stuck inside this darkness.
I need to stand up,
For myself and my heart.
Even if evil stands against me,
May this wish soar towards the sky,
And land on my happiness."

AS THE YEARS WENT BY, the curse that distressed Princess Chenoa had turned into a significant weight on her heart. A large number of evenings, she changed into the fearsome mythical beast, her delicate soul caught inside the sturdy chamber. The information on her curse was known exclusively to her dad, King Aryan, who bore the heaviness of this mystery with overwhelming sadness.

One afternoon, King Aryan assembled his kids in the royal residence's fantastic corridor. The brilliant beams of the sunset washed the room, projecting a warm shine over the family as they arranged to examine matters of the kingdom. In any case, Princess Chenoa's mind was occupied with the longing to break free from her cursed destiny.

As the royal advisor introduced his report on the kingdom's issues, Princess Chenoa's thoughts floated to a story she had heard about a voyaging storyteller from him. The story discussed a young fellow who had coincidentally found a cavern occupied by an old wise hermit for granting any wish. Looking for that old hermit in order to break her curse ignited a promise of something better inside her heart. She had to find him fast.

Without containing her interest and franticness any longer, Chenoa gathered her courage to make a request. "Father," she started reluctantly, "I have heard a story of an old wise hermit whom able to grant wishes. Do you suppose such an individual really exists?"

King Aryan checked out at his little girl with concern, noticing the unrest in her spirit. "Indeed, my dear, there are legends of strong hermits who have such powers," he answered delicately.

Chenoa then took a full breath prior uncovering her deepest desire. "Father, I wish to track down this person and look for his guidance to break the curse that has been plaguing me."

Nonetheless, the King's face turned harsh, and his voice conveyed a hint of misery. "My cherished girl, I figure out your desire, yet it is unreasonably dangerous. Imagine a scenario in where the old hermit can't be found, or more terribly, on the off chance that he gives a wish that brings more bad luck than anything."

Princess Chenoa's eyes gushed with tears of disappointment and yearning. "Father, I can't bear this curse any more. I'm willing to face the challenge and face the outcomes. Kindly accept my appeal."

A mixture of concern and fatherly love filled King Aryan's heart as he considered his girl's mournful eyes. After a moment of pondering, he talked with a heavy sigh, "Alright, my dear. I see the assurance in your heart. However, guarantee me that you will be wary and come to me right away assuming anything turns out badly." Princess Chenoa's face illuminated with appreciation, and she embraced her dad firmly. "Much thanks to you, Father. Your affection and support mean everything to me."

That next morning, Chenoa arranged to leave on her dangerous trip to track down the old wise hermit. She wore a basic shroud to mask her regal identity and got out of the royal residence, her heart loaded up with trust and fear.

Unaware about the difficulties waiting for her, Princess Chenoa ventured into the unknown in order to be liberated from the curse which had tormented her for a really long time. Much to her dismay that her journey would be filled with unexpected experiences and significant revelations, driving her towards a fate far more noteworthy than she could ever imagine.

"I need to do this..." she said nervously.

"Be brave and strong myself," she continued.

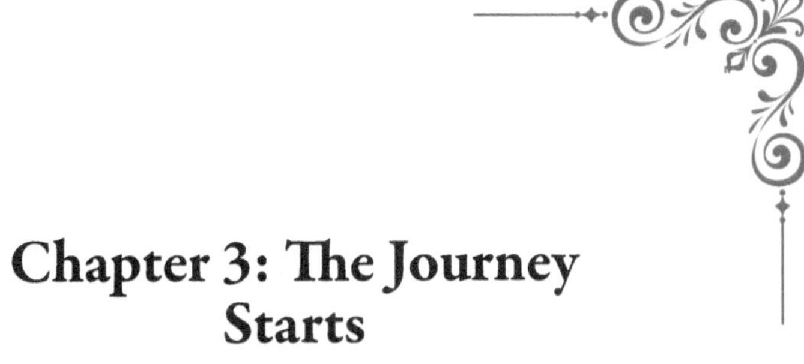

Chapter 3: The Journey Starts

"I walk and keep walking,
Even if they stare at me, I will keep blinking my eyes, unfazed,
For my fate will neither waver nor wane,
It will change someday, I'm certain."

UNDER THE SHIMMERING light of the sun, Princess Chenoa wandered into the huge and puzzling woodland encompassing the kingdom. The stirring leaves and tormenting calls of night animals reverberated through the thick foliage as she strolled warily, her heart thumping with both dedication and anxiety.

With each step, her resolve developed further. She was determined to track down the old hermit loner and break the curse that tormented her. The memory of her dad's fair warnings lingered in her head, yet she realized that she needed to face this challenge, for the burden of the curse had become unbearable.

As the hours passed, the woodland appeared to develop considerably hazier and more unaccustomed. Princess Chenoa's steps wavered, and doubt started to crawl into her heart. She contemplated whether she was silly to trust in the stories of an old hermit who could give wishes.

As uncertainty was about to overwhelm her, a soft glow grabbed her eye. Following the ethereal light, she coincidentally found a wounded deer, its eyes reflecting torment and weakness. Moved by empathy, Chenoa approached slowly toward the injured animal.

Delicately kneeling close to the deer, she murmured relieving words as she reached out her hand to touch its harmed leg. The deer looked into her eyes as though grasping her kind intention. "Dread not, respectable animal," she murmured, "I will attempt to help you."

Closing her eyes, Chenoa directed the enchantment inside her that she had kept concealed for such a long time. A delicate, brilliant light encompassed her hand as she laid them on the deer's injury. Gradually, the injury started to recover, and the deer's strength returned.

" Now, in your restored wholeness, my dear deer, run with swiftness akin to flight, as if you could soar and capture the very essence of the sky." Chenoa said to the deer.

Thankful, the deer bowed its head prior to running away into the woods. Chenoa smiled, feeling a recharged sense of purpose. Maybe her sympathy and readiness to help others would lead her to the old hermit she looked for.

As she proceeded with her journey, she came across another injured creature. This time, it was a visually impaired hare battling to track down its direction through the undergrowth. Chenoa couldn't tolerate leaving the unfortunate animal vulnerable, so she carefully directed it into somewhere safe. Yet again her secret enchantment worked its marvels, and the hare's sight was supernaturally restored.

"Behold, small creature, your vision is restored. Gaze upon the resplendent blossoms; their beauty is a testament to nature's grace. I pray that with your renewed sight, you may forever perceive the kindness within the human heart." She whispered and then smiled as she was satisfied.

The hare jumped away, leaving Chenoa awestruck by the force of her own powers. She had never completely embraced her otherworldly gifts, fearing that they would affect one way or another to the curse within her. Nonetheless, this evening of aiding animals in need had made her realized that her magic was a gift to be utilized for good deeds forever.

As sunrise drew closer, Princess Chenoa's assurance to find the old hermit just grew more. The preliminaries she experienced on the way had fortified her conviction that there was still goodness and trust on the planet. She realized that she was destined to break liberated from the curse and, in doing as such, achieve positive change for her and others.

With a newly discovered feeling of direction, Princess Chenoa proceeded with her excursion, directed by the illumination of the rising sun and the faithful expectation in her heart. Much to her dismay that her experiences with the injured deer and the visually impaired bunny were just the start of a significant and extraordinary journey that would lead her to the responses she looked for and the real essence of her predetermination.

Chapter 4: The Experience
with the Wise Hermit

"Dear heaven, I sing my heartbreak lullaby,
Will my sadness vanish? Please tell me, someday, yes it will.
Even the night comes to an end,
Even the rain will cease,
This pain will fade away someday."

AS PRINCESS CHENOA ventured further into the woodland, she experienced different difficulties and moments of self-disclosure. Her heart expanded with both assurance and freshly discovered comprehension of her otherworldly powers. With each thoughtful gesture towards the unfortunate animals, her confidence developed, and she felt more connected with the world around her.

As the sun hit its peak, she unexpectedly found a beautiful field embellished with colorful wildflowers. There, an injured sparrow laying on the grass, its fragile wing twisted at an unnatural condition. Princess Chenoa's heart went out to the little bird, and she realized she needed to help it.

Gently carrying the sparrow, she supported it in her grasp and murmured soothing words. Her magical healing ability encompassed into the little animal, and a warm brilliant light washed away the blood of its injured wing. Yet again gradually, the wing got fixed, and the sparrow tweeted euphorically, flying-off into the sky.

" Soar, little sparrow, with dreams as boundless as the sky. May your wings carry you to the haven of happiness and guide you to your destined sanctuary." Chenoa said to the sparrow, hoping everything would be fine.

Appreciatively, the sparrow hovering above prior to arriving on her shoulder. Chenoa grinned, understanding that these experiences with harmed animals were not merely accidental events. They were actually directing her towards something far more important - perhaps even directly to the old hermit she had been looking for.

As dusk drew nearer, Chenoa felt a combination of weariness and assurance. She looked for shelter in a little cavern at the edge of the woodland, whereby she turned herself into a dragon for that evening. Isolating herself from outsiders, strangely calm staying inside. At the back of her mind, while laying and gazing at the stars through the cavern's opened ceiling's hole right near above her head, her contemplations floated back in about her family and her dad's advice. She later dozed off and slept throughout the night.

"I hope Father understands the reason why I needed to do this," she said to herself. "I can't bear this curse any more, and I should figure out how to break it. Fast."

The following morning, revived by a night's rest, Chenoa proceeded with her journey. Her steps were guided by an internal compass - an instinct. It drove her deeper into the core of the woods. She could feel that she was moving nearer towards her objective, and her eagerness blended with anxious expectation.

At long last, she suddenly found a clear opened area where a mystical aura appeared to be consuming the space in the forest. In the center of the place, stood there an old giant oak tree. Its monstrous branches coming out towards the sky. She saw magical creatures turned into pink colored glowing flowers – Golden peacocks transformed into illuminating water lilies on a pond near the big tree. There was a small waterfall nearby the tree too. She then looked down under the tree and saw a respected figure – an old man. It's the wise hermit.

His eyes were glimmered with pool of joy, and a peaceful grin graced his tired face. Princess Chenoa moved toward him consciously, her heart beating with both nervousness and trust.

"Hello there, dear wise elder," she said with a quiver in her voice. "I'm Princess Chenoa and I came here asking for your advice." Chenoa introduced herself.

The old hermit's eyes met hers with a knowing look, and he greeted back kindly. "Welcome, Princess Chenoa, I have already detected your presence well before you showed up in front of me. Tell me, what is the reason for your tiring quest?"

With a blend of fear and assurance, Chenoa shared her situation, the curse that transformed her into a winged serpent, dragon, every night and her wish was to be utterly liberated from its painful grasp. She discussed her experiences with the harmed animals and her conviction that those chain of events had driven her to him.

The old hermit listened mindfully, his presence quieting her restless soul. "Your journey has not been an entirely waste, Princess," he answered, his voice filled with sympathy. "It is true upon the case that I have the ability to grant any wishes, however, the fulfillment of those wishes not just lies in my grasp, but also within your heart."

He signaled his hand to her to sit before him, and as she did, he proceeded, "You have displayed extraordinary kindness and selflessness, utilizing your enchanted gifts to help those who were hurt and in need. Your heart is sacred, and it is through this sacredness truly lies the key for breaking the curse, Princess".

Chenoa listened attentively, retaining his words like a thirsty soul in a scorching hot oasis desert. The old man's insight echoed profoundly inside her, and she understood that the answer for her curse was not a mystical chant but rather a comprehension of herself and her purpose.

"Understood," she said with her firm voice of a newly discovered clarity. "I should embrace my magic and use it to help other people, to be a power of good on this world."

The wise old man nodded affirmatively. "Certainly, Princess. Your mystical gifts are actually a reflection of your sympathy and compassion. Embrace them, and your true destiny shall be uncovered."

With appreciation in her heart, Chenoa expressed gratitude toward the old wise hermit for his advice. As she bid him farewell and moved back from the place, she felt a newly discovered feeling of direction and determination. She realized that her journey had recently started, and that embracing her enchanted gifts was the only way to fully unlock her actual potential.

With her heart filled up with hope and resolve, Princess Chenoa left onto the next stage of her journey - to embrace her magic and use it to help other people, realizing that it was not only her curse that should have been broken, yet the boundaries that tied off her from completely understanding her fate.

Chapter 5: A Path of Self-Revelation

"The darkness will surely end, trust me,
For I've heard it from those who've seen it before,
They've walked through the shadows, just as you and I.
Like a sunflower, plucked and yet, another blooms,
Nature's eternal reminder that life persists, even until the world's final
embrace."

WITH THE OLD WISE HERMIT'S guidance and freshly discovered purpose in her heart, Princess Chenoa proceeded with her journey with a feeling of clear direction and determination. She wandered further into the woods, utilizing her supernatural capacities to help unfortunate animals along on the way. Every act of kindness, strengthened her confidence in the belief of compassion and shaping her own destiny.

As she crossed through the captivated woods, words of the kind princess who had mystical healing abilities started to spread among the creatures. Birds praised her joyfully, and forest animals rose up out of their hiding places to look for her help. Chenoa kept an eye on each animal with adoration and care, realizing that her actions held the only key to breaking her curse.

At some point, as she was resting by a calm stream, a modest hedgehog moved toward her with a quake in its voice. "Princess, I have gone far to look for your guide," the hedgehog said with appreciation in its eyes. "My young ones are caught in a dangerous cave. Please, will you help them?"

"Yes, I will, show me the way." She replied.

Princess Chenoa's heart expanded with empathy, and she promptly consented to help. Following the hedgehog's directions, she wandered into the dim and narrowed cave. Guided by her magical light, she found the young hedgehogs huddled together in distress.

With delicate hands and a consoling presence, Chenoa helped every hedgehog to somewhere safe and secure, driving them out of the cave. The hedgehog family offered their thanks with blissful squeaks, their little eyes sparkling with gratefulness.

"Release your burdens, break free from the shadowy cell of distress, and may the radiant embrace of light eternally find its way to you." Chenoa was satisfied with her help.

As news of her deeds spread further, different animals looked for her guide. A lost young bear found its direction back to its mom's hug, a group of wolves were saved from a furious river, and a harmed birds had its fragile wings fixed. Each experience carried her nearer to figuring out the real nature of her magical gifts.

Yet, in the midst of the delight and satisfaction of helping other people, a lingering doubt distressed her spirit. Could these kind gestures really be sufficient to break the curse that tormented her? As the sun plunged beneath the skyline one night, Chenoa ended up pondering her way. Again, in a beastly form laying inside her cave.

Sitting under a shade of stars, she spilled her guts to the night sky, looking for comfort in the quietness of the forest. "Am I doing what's needed?" she whispered. "Will my kindness be the only way to breaking this curse, or am I bound to be caught in the darkness for eternity?"

At that time of weakness, a delicate breeze stirred the leaves over her. It seemed like nature's reaction, a soothing consolation that her journey held a reason far more superior than she could understand.

As the days transformed into weeks, her thoughtful gestures continued, touching the existences of countless animals. Each act conveyed with it a freshly discovered comprehension of her wizardry and the acknowledgment that compassion was also a force of transformation within oneself.

"Dear Divine, may you soothe the tumultuous waves of my heart, for this relentless anxiety plagues my every moment. Yet, with unwavering resolve, I yearn to conquer it through the wellspring of my inner strength, though, at times, it eludes me. I implore you, O Beloved, to grant me the fortitude of your boundless grace. Dispel my worries, shatter the curse that binds me, and usher serenity into the depths of my troubled mind." Chenoa whispered straight into her heart.

One night, as the moon rose up high in the sky, Chenoa in a dragon form, suddenly felt a flood of energy flowing through her. The forest appeared to wake up with a magical aura, and a strong presence encompassed her. Her heart was glowing with a green warm light. Slowly turning her into a human form momentarily. The answer that she had been looking for was inside her all along.

Tears of acknowledgment gushed down her cheeks as she comprehended that the genuine key to breaking the curse was not only her graciousness towards others, but also towards herself. By embracing her magical gifts and involving them for good, she was breaking the barriers that had held her back for such a long time.

With newly discovered self-acknowledgment and love, Princess Chenoa promised to proceed with her journey of sympathy, realizing that she was breaking her curse, yet changing her destiny. As she gazed toward the moon, she realized that her story was nowhere near finished, and that her heart would direct her towards a fate, greater than she could have ever possibly imagined.

Chapter 6: Embracing Destiny

"You and I, we are but human after all,
Even if seven worlds despise me,
As long as it's not the skies,
Not the Owner of the universe,
We will find our way, just fine."

WITH RECENTLY DISCOVERED clarity and self-acknowledgment, Princess Chenoa's journey took on a deeper meaning. Each thoughtful gesture, both towards others and herself, turned into a demonstration of the force of empathy and the strength laying inside her heart. As she kept on going through the magical forest, her reputation as the big-hearted princess with mystical healing power spread all over, arriving at the farthest corners of the kingdom.

At some point, as she moved toward an interesting town on the edges of the woods, the locals hurried to welcome her with appreciation and love. They had heard stories of her wonderful deeds, and they had come to look for her help. She healed those people who were ill, restored broken bones, and carried trust and recovering to all different kinds of sick people who looked for her.

In any case, in the midst of the love, Princess Chenoa's heart stayed humble and grounded. She realized that the genuine source of her power was not her mystical power, but rather the sympathy and love that moved through her. With every individual she helped, she saw their spirits got lifted, and hope was revived in their eyes.

As the days turned into weeks, rumors of her healing power finally arrived at the palace, and King Aryan got insight about this kind princess travelling in the kingdom. The narratives were not new to him, and a hint of something better over the horizon started inside his heart. He couldn't resist the opportunity to contemplate whether this princess could be, as a matter of fact, his cherished little girl, Princess Chenoa.

Driven by interest and a father's yearning, King Aryan disguised himself as an random voyager and set out to track down this secretive healer. As he moved toward the town, he saw the noteworthy scenes of empathy and healing done by the altruistic princess.

Attracted to the spirit of kindness that encompassed her, King Aryan felt a feeling of familiarity as he noticed her interactions with the locals. He watched with awe as she embraced her mystical gifts, utilizing them to acquire bliss and relief to those need.

Later in the afternoon, as she sat under the shade of a tree, watching out for an injured bird, King Aryan moved toward her with fear, uncertain on the off chance that his doubts were right. "Excuse me, kind healer," he said, his voice shaking with feeling, "May I talk with you?"

Chenoa gazed upward, and her eyes met those of the disguised King. There was a gleam of acknowledgment, and her heart skirted a thump. "Obviously," she answered energetically, welcoming him to sit next to her.

As they spoke, King Aryan was filled with both joy and sadness, for he realized that this merciful healer was for sure his long missing daughter. His heart swelled proudly at the amazing lady she had become, yet it pounded with the information on the weight she had carried alone.

In a moment of weakness, Chenoa trusted the voyager, sharing her journey to break the curse that had tormented her. King Aryan listened eagerly yet his heart felt broken for his girl's struggles.

"My dear, you are genuinely a guide of light and trust," he expressed, unfit to contain his feelings any longer. "Your consideration and sympathy have touched the existences of so many, and I'm so proud to call you as my daughter."

Tears rolled down Princess Chenoa's cheeks, and she embraced her dad, feeling a sense of belonging and love she had longed for such an extremely long time. The heaviness of her mystery lifted as she shared her journey and the acknowledgment of her fate with King Aryan.

With reality uncovered, King Aryan embraced his little girl's actual personality, as of now not troubled by the need to keep quiet. The bond among father and girl developed considerably further as they set out on another chapter of their lives together. While his kingdom was being handled by his son, Prince Joshua.

In the following day, Chenoa proceeded with her healing journey, presently now joined by her father, King Aryan, who was humbled by his little girl's strength, compassion and wisdom. The kingdom commended the arrival of their adored princess, presently known for her loyal legacy as well as for her sympathetic heart and magical gifts.

As the sun set on another captivating day, Princess Chenoa understood that her mission to break the curse was undeniably more beyond her imagination. It wasn't just about liberating herself from a spell, however about finding her actual reason and embracing her fate as a source point of sympathy and love on the planet. Thus, she ventured forward with her father close by, prepared to confront anything challenges lay ahead, realizing that the force of consideration and love would lead her towards a greater fate that was more prominent than any curse or charm.

" Dearest heart of mine, my precious daughter, I stand before you, ready to unite our souls. Together, we shall weave a tapestry of serenity across this world, akin to the harmonious dance of river and sea. Our voyage is a pilgrimage of self-discovery, an expedition to shatter the shackles of malevolence with the radiance of benevolence. And one day, mark my words, our dream shall echo through the cosmos, a resplendent beacon of hope for all." He said it with tears in his eyes. Chenoa then held her father's hand tight and said, "Let's do this, father."

Chapter 7: Untying Facts

"Why do you rush so, my friend,
When the sky above gazes upon your journey?
Pause, for even the heavens themselves take their time,
To observe the stories of those who traverse this world."

AS PRINCESS CHENOA and King Aryan proceeded with their journey together, their bond strengthened as time passed. The kingdom greeted its beloved princess back wholeheartedly, celebrating her return and embracing her newly discovered goal as a healer and an encouraging hope.

Amidst of their journey, the wise hermit's words echoed in Princess Chenoa's mind. She knew that her journey to break the curse was not entirely about her own freedom but rather about embracing her enchanted gifts and utilizing them to have an effect in the existences of others. Her heart filled with appreciation for the hermit's direction, for it had driven her to this significant acknowledgment.

As they wandered through the kingdom, healing unfortunate ones, they came across a little kid who had lost herself in the forest. The young lady's eyes were filled with anxiety, and she gripped a locket firmly to her chest. Chenoa gently moved toward her, offering a comforting smile and a consoling hand.

"Hello dear" she said merciful. "I'm Princess Chenoa, and this is my dad, King Aryan. We're here to help you. May you please tell us know your name?"

The young lady hesitated a bit but spoke in low voice, "I am Mary. I-I'm lost, and I can't see as my way home."

With a gentle touch, Chenoa wiped away Mary's tears and offered her hand. "Sit back and relax, Mary. We'll assist you finding your way back home. Here. Simply hold my hand, and we'll go together."

As they strolled through the grassland, Mary's hold on the locket to her chest, and curiosity got the better of Princess Chenoa. "Is there something particularly important about that locket, Mary?" she asked.

Mary gestured shyly, said in a low voice. "It's a locket that my grandma gave me before she died. She said it holds a unique mystery that can safeguard me, yet I don't have any idea how to open it."

Captivated, Chenoa inspected the memento, seeing complex inscriptions of magical symbols. The acknowledgment struck her that this locket could hold a secret power. With her magical detection's skill, she noticed a weak aura emanating from the locket, showing its definitely an importance piece of item.

"Would you like me to attempt to open it for you?" Chenoa offered, her heart wavering with eagerness.

Mary's eyes widened in amazement and trust. "Could you at any point do that, Princess?"

With a nod, Chenoa channeled in her magical energy on the locket. The engravings gleamed faintly, answering her touch. Gradually, the locked clicked open, uncovering a little, sparkling precious stone settled inside.

Mary panted in awe, and her face illuminated with gratitude. "It's gorgeous! What is it?"

"It's a magical gem," Chenoa made sense of. "What's more, it seems that it is resonating by your grandma's love and protection. Keep it near your heart, and it will look after you, directing you back to somewhere safe at whatever point you feel lost."

Mary embraced Princess Chenoa, appreciation spilling over in her heart. "Much thanks to you, Princess. That is truly wonderful!"

With a smile, Chenoa answered, "We all have a bit of magic inside us, Mary. It's the abundance and sympathy we share with others that make the world a better place."

As they bid goodbye to Mary, King Aryan looked at his girl with admiration and pride. He had seen her enchanted gifts and the significant effect she had on individuals' lives, and he realized that her fate as a healer and a compassionate leader was unfolding before his eyes.

As the sun rose on another day, Princess Chenoa and King Aryan proceeded with their journey, touching the souls of many in need. Every act of kindness made, they brought in more healing and hope to the kingdom, planting the seeds of positive change.

Little did they know that their journey was nowhere near finished, for there were still many privileged insights and difficulties waiting for them. However, they confronted the unknown with courage and love, realizing that their hearts were joined in their mission to create a world where benevolence and sympathy ruled, and where magic was a fantastical story as well as an unstoppable power that gave joy and healing to all. Thus, they marched through hand in hand, prepared to embrace anything that destiny had coming up for them, realizing that the force of love and magic would lead them towards a future laid with hope and endless possibilities.

Chapter 8: The Magical Forest

"In the realm of the magical heart,
Even amidst the black rose's thorns,
Evil's cease draws near,
As it beholds the shimmering white rose's edge,
As people look on,
Evil's defeat and doom are sealed."

AS PRINCESS CHENOA and King Aryan wandered further into the kingdom, they heard murmurs of an old and baffling woodland that held untold secrets and charms. The stories discussed where magic streamed like a waterway and where people entered and came out everlastingly different. Captivated by the narratives and looking for replies, they chose to investigate the amazing Magical Forest.

The forest invited them with an ethereal beauty, trees embellished with brilliant blossoms transmitted a delicate light. As they dove further into the forest's heart, a feeling of miracle and awe washed over them, and they realized that this place was unlike any other they had experienced before.

"Isn't it beautiful? Sound of peace," she said.

"Yes, my dear princess, the melody comes straight into my heart," King Aryan replied.

They were listening to it; it was a very soothing and calming sound.

As they moved towards, they met many enchanted animals and experienced otherworldly peculiarities past their imagination. Wisps of light moved in the air, and the forest appeared to whisper mysteries in a language no one but they could comprehend. Princess Chenoa 's magical senses shivered with eagerness, and she felt a significant association with the essence of the forest.

In the core of the Magical Forest, they coincidentally found an old stone platform with a gleaming crystal settling upon it. The crystal beat with an extraordinary light, and King Aryan remembered it as the very sort of precious stone that had been inside Mary's memento.

"What happened?" she asked.

"I don't know, but I know there's something in it," he said, nervously thinking about what was happening. King Aryan held his daughter's hand. She held his hand strongly.

They got really curious. They reached out slowly and touched the precious stone at the same time. Immediately, a strong flood of magic surged through them, encompassing them in a glorious light. They felt as though they were converging with the essence of the forest itself timberland, becoming one with its magic.

In this magical realm, they saw dreams of their past, present, and future. King Aryan saw the distress he had conveyed for quite a long time, the minutes he had missed with his girl, and the problems he had brought about by staying quiet. He promised to set things straight and to be the father that Chenoa truly deserved.

Princess Chenoa, in her vision, saw the strength inside her, the love she conveyed in her heart, and the significant effect of her kindness had on others. She comprehended that her magical gifts were not a curse but rather a blessing, intended to be shared to the world. Embracing her destiny, she promised to keep spreading love and healing any place she went.

As the dreams stopped, they ended up back in the present, their hands actually entwined with the precious stone's wizardry. They realized that this experience had been no mere coincidence; it was a revelation of their actual selves and the interconnectedness of their destinies.

"Do you see what I see, dad? She asked.

"Yes, my dear, you need to embrace it into your mind and your little heart," King Aryan expressed with worry.

She cried by remembering her struggle in the past. As a cursed dragon creature, it was so troubling to her heart and made her anxious all the time. King Aryan knew what's in little his daughter's heart and said "Chenoa my dear daughter, be patient and calm yourself, soon miracle will come, endure it a little longer, I know it's difficult for you but I also know, you will overcome this, we will do this together, with faith and prayer, this will come to end." He tried to sooth his daughter. Princess Chenoa wiped her tears and hugged her father. It was full of family's love. If her father believed it so did her. She needed to believe in herself. Anything is possible by being blessed from this universe. For what she saw in her vision, she believed it would happen someday.

With newly discovered clarity and a feeling of unity, they chose to bring that precious stone with them, representing the magic within them and their obligation to spread love and kindness. The stone gleamed with a warm radiance, reflecting the affection that bound them together.

As they left the Magical Forest, they felt changed, changed by the magic that had embraced them. Their journey had become more significant, and they realized that their destinies were tied with the fate of the kingdom and every one of its people.

After getting back to the kingdom, Chenoa and King Aryan shared their encounters with Prince Joshua and their people. The legend of the Magical Forest grew even more deeper. They urged others to accept their inner magic, to look past appearances and see the beauty and potential in each soul.

The kingdom flourished under their joint rule, with love and kindness as their core values in making every choice. The magical of the

Magical Forest had contacted them as well as all who lived there, making a realm of understanding and harmony. After they shared their vision and mission, they continued their journey.

As they proceeded with their next journey, guided by the precious stone's light and the love in their souls, Princess Chenoa and King Aryan knew that the way forward would be filled up with many challenges and trials. However, they went through the future with courage, realizing that they were joined by a bond stronger than any curse or magic - the magic of love and the power of kindness, which been able to impact the world each act of good deeds in turn.

Chapter 9: The Beginnings of Unity

"Each dawn heralds a fresh day,
With new hopes that gently sway,
A renewed mind, ready to convey,
Opportunities anew, in life's grand ballet."

AS PRINCESS CHENOA and King Aryan continued with their journey, they experienced new difficulties that tested their unity and obligation to their common purpose. The Magical Forest's magic had reinforced their bond, yet it also put them into trials which they needed to confront together.

One such test emerged when they went over a town plagued by conflicts and disagreement. The locals were divided by old complaints, and harshness had been rooted in their souls. Princess Chenoa and King Aryan saw that their test had gone beyond healing physical injuries; they needed to heal the wounds of the spirit – emotional injuries.

With unwavering assurance, they hustled hard to unite the residents through demonstrations of love and kindness. They coordinated common social occasions, where stories were shared, and forgiveness was looked for. Gradually and steadily, the hearts of the locals started to calm down, and the seeds of unity were planted.

Nonetheless, not every person embraced the message of love, and they confronted resistance from the people who stuck to their hatred and anger. Princess Chenoa's purpose was tested; however, she recalled the old wise man's words about the force of kindness and that change would require more time and efforts.

Despite affliction, King Aryan remained by his daughter's side, offering his faithful help and advice. Together, they stood up to the difficulties with courage and love, looking for same perspective in the midst of difference point of views.

As days turned into weeks, the town gradually changed, and the divisions started to disappear. The force of their love and kindness rose above the hindrances that had once isolated the residents. Harmony and peace replaced hatred, and the town turned into a beacon light of hope for the whole kingdom.

Nonetheless, their journey and it wasn't without personal struggles. King Aryan fought with responsibility for having kept Princess Chenoa's actual identity concealed for such a long time, yet she consoled him that their recently discovered unity was a demonstration of the healing power of love.

As they wandered further, one day, they suddenly encountered a dark power that threatened the harmony they had worked really hard to accomplish. An evil witch, envious of Princess Chenoa 's magical gifts, sought to steal away her powers to reinforce her own dark magic.

That one day drastically turned into the night, and the place changed into a desert full of red thorn cactus. People were running away with their frightened hearts. The evil witch spoke loudly from the skies.

"My, oh my, dear, my cursed princess....", she said it with a sarcastic voice.

"It's you!" said King Aryan angrily.

King Aryan tried to kill her with his sword. But the evil witch turned into a mist, and suddenly she was right behind his back. King Aryan tried to turn back, but she attacked him with her red-light magic. All his armies were trying to help, but she casted a spell and bound them with her roots.

"Father!" Chenoa tried to help but couldn't move. Chenoa tried to unseal her magic, but it was no use.

"Chenoa!" the king called her loudly.

"Even you are human right now, but how pity; you are just a despicable creature; you are useless!" the evil witch then laughed hysterically.

"You!" King Aryan tried to get up, but he couldn't.

"Do you remember King Aryan? Our memories, yes, our beautiful memories of being together...," she said.

"Leona," she said again.

In the past, they were young teenagers, and they were best friends. King Aryan, Leona, and Athena. Together, they helped people and killed many monsters that disturbed them. They had found this magical land, which was beautiful and peaceful. Full of flying golden feathers and flowers, the animals were looking so miraculous that these three best friends explored them with full curiosity. Immediately, they found something hiding behind the magical cave: a gemstone. It was so shining, like a beam of light from the sun.

King Aryan was trying to pull it out when, all of a sudden, the cave was shaking. They ran out together with a million steps. They were so panicked. The cave had collapsed, and they watched it together, almost out of breath. Even though the magical cave collapsed but not the gemstone, it was already in his hand. He knew there was something in it that was so special.

They named the land, Ankaa, with the gemstone King Aryan was in a powerful state; he was becoming stronger than ever. However, one day, something unexpected happened. When King Aryan, Leona, and Athena were trying to help their town, it suddenly turned into a devastated state where the enemies intruded. The enemy, Black Knight was very strong. King Aryan was trying to fight him but couldn't. He felt weakness in him when he was trying to face him. "Why?!?" King Aryan was trying to figure it out. Why his gemstone was not working.

The Black Knight was trying to push the sword towards King Aryan, but it didn't work because, it was Leona; she got stabbed instead. She was trying to protect him, King Aryan was screaming full of anger. He gave a heavy blow onto the Black Knight, and he managed to knock him out, collapsed. He called out Leona's name repeatedly but she told them to leave immediately because the other knights were coming.

" Aryan... It is no use. He is too strong to be defeated. Please go now for God's sake. Go with Athena..." Leona was trying to talk to him in that devastated state.

"No, Leona, our kids are waiting for us. You need to survive. You need to live; how am I going to live without you, Leona?" King Aryan was crying for help.

"No, please go for now... You need to go... Our people need us. If you are killed with Athena, who is going to protect our people and our kids?" Leona was trying to talk, but it was so difficult for her.

"No..," King Aryan was heartbroken. He couldn't leave her just like that.

At their back, the other enemies were running towards them. The Black Knight was trying to get up and took his sword.

"This is my last word; our people need you, and so do our dear children need their dad. Goodbye for now. My dear king, my love." Those were her last words.

Athena was trying to help, but it was too late. Leona was gone. This time, Athena was taking some actions; she pulled his arm up and brought them both onto the carriage. They were leaving the scene. The Black Knight just stood there like a statue, watching them silently. Like he was hiding something. In the unknown forest, Leona was buried by her husband, King Aryan, with the help of Athena. They were mourning together for their beloved love and friend.

That night, King Aryan was having a strange dream; it was almost a vision. A strange dragon creature was flying across the moon. He was awake. Then suddenly, he heard something from behind the big oak tree. It was Athena, and someone was talking.

"Even though now he was sad, soon or later, I will support him with full of compassion; he will eventually be mine, here now yours." Athena was giving the person something. It looked like a token of appreciation—the diamonds.

Surprisingly, it was the Black Knight. "What?! but why?" King Aryan couldn't hold himself.

"Athena!!! Why did you do this?!," King Aryan pulled his sword with his anger towards them.

"My, are you awake? Did we wake you up? Oh no, my apology," said Athena with her wicked smile.

"Why, Athena, after all we have been through, why did you do this? Why, Athena?" King Aryan asked.

"I have to!" she replied.

"Huh?!," King Aryan couldn't believe what he saw.

"Because I love you, King Aryan," she then said.

"No, it couldn't be," he replied.

"You know, I am also a woman. But you guys always make me feel like an unimportant person. I'm always in the middle. I could feel that I'm just interrupting you both; Leona was everything while you always make me as nothing!" she explained it with anger in herself.

"Don't say her name with your wicked mouth." King Aryan was pushing his sword towards her, but the Black Knight was protecting Athena. Athena was laughing wickedly.

"Why are you changing Athena?" King Aryan felt unsatisfied with what he witnessed. King Aryan was pulling to his pocket and took his gemstone on his palm. He was hoping for his gemstone's miracle. But it wasn't shining.

"That was a fake gemstone, my dear." Athena was laughing to see him look like that.

"What!?" he exhaled.

"With this in my hand, everything will be possible. I'm strong, King Aryan, and I will always be!" She then laughed and turned into the dragon creature. King Aryan was panicking; he couldn't believe what was happening. Why his friend was turning into that monster. He couldn't believe his eyes.

"I've been looking for this gemstone for centuries! Thank you for finding me this, dear King!" she said wickedly.

"Who are you?", King Aryan asked.

"I am the wicked and cursed evil witch. Athena Salazar!!! After all these years, I can't pull this thing off. Thank you for lending me your hand, Aryan; now it's mine!" she laughed again.

"I can't get you, but I'm having this!" and ... I'm leaving my present to your daughter! She will be the next curse!" She spoke sarcastically, then flew away from him. King Aryan was out of his breath; he was too panicked for what was happening and trying to run as fast as he could to figure out the meaning of leaving her present to her daughter was, but then out of his breath, he collapsed while trying to get to his children.

His wife was gone, as was the magical land of Ankaa. It turned into a desert. The magical land lost its magical power.

"Because of you, Leona was gone, you evil witch!" King Aryan was running again towards Athena. But Athena turned again into the mist.

"I think you need to know this, your son, Prince Joshua, already gone too," she said with wicked smile. She then appeared at their back.

King Aryan couldn't hold back his anger. He almost exploded into wrath upon hearing those words. He was also so sad to hear of his son's death. He wanted to attack her with all his madness.

"Father, let me," Princess Chenoa was holding herself. After what she heard, she was angry, but she was trying to control herself. Now she knows her enemy—the one that was turning her into the dragon creature.

She was having a flashback to all of her trials and happiness at healing people, animals and...her mother, her brother. Now, she had to fight it until the end.

Athena released powerful dark spells and illusions, testing Princess Chenoa's magical powers. Regardless, with King Aryan by Princess Chenoa's side close by, offering relentless help and protection, Chenoa tapped deeper into her magical powers. She channeled the feelings of love and kindness inside her to counter-attack the darkness, knowing that the true magic was not about that destroying evil but rather creating good and peace.

Their fight against the evil witch was wild, yet the strength of their unity won. Together, they harnessed the force of love and kindness, scattering the hatred and turning the evil witch towards path of redemption.

With the evil witch got transformed by the healing power of love, Athena couldn't resist. Princess Chenoa and King Aryan showed that even the most stoned-cold hearts, it could be moved by love and kindness.

Athena, the evil witch turned into mist, she was defeated and gone forever.

As they proceeded with their journey, they experienced more villages needing healing and more difficulties. Every test brought them closer, and their hearts stayed firm in their mission to spread love and kindness all through the kingdom.

With each act of kindness, they witnessed the extraordinary power of unity that their fate was to break the curse as well as to create a world where kindness and love ruled.

As they traveled forward together, Princess Chenoa and King Aryan felt that their bond was getting stronger over time. They had beaten trials and difficulties, arising as symbols of love and kindness, joined in their responsibility to make the kingdom a position of harmony and peace.

Their story was nowhere near finished, however they walked forward with reestablished courage and hope, accepting that the power of love could overcome any evil darkness and that together, they would keep on spreading the magic of kindness, one step at a time.

Chapter 10: The Discovery

"Within this sadness, I craft happiness,
In harmony with the universe, my heart composes verse,
Not in opposition to you, but in reflection of the journey within me."

AS PRINCESS CHENOA and King Aryan proceeded with their journey, they came across a town settled at the foot of a majestic mountain. The townspeople greeted them wholeheartedly, and the air was filled with warmth and joy. However, as they spent more time with the townspeople, they sensed a sadness that covered like a cloak over the town.

"This town is crying; I knew there's something breaking their hearts; it's surrounded by darkness," Chenoa said confidentially, looking at the atmosphere.

"We need seek the truth of what's going on," said King Aryan.

Both of them got curious, and they investigated to reveal the main source of the town's despair. Later, they learned of a legend that had tormented the town for ages - The Legend of The Breaking Mountain. It was said that the mountain sobbed tears of gemstones at whatever point it sensed the presence of true love.

"This true love has been broken inside; it's filled with sadness as if it's being separated from kindness," Chenoa said.

Intrigued, Princess Chenoa and King Aryan chose to climb the Breaking Mountain, anxious to observe this supernatural mystery. As they got over, the air became colder, and the mountain appeared to echo with whispers of sorrow.

At the highest peak, they were met with a stunning view. The mountain's peak was covered with flickering gemstones that looked like tears, sparkling under the morning glow. The legend had confirmed it's tale, yet it left them with more questions than answers.

With a delicate touch, Chenoa reached out the precious gemstones, sensing a strong surge of emotion. A dream overflowed her brain, uncovering a romantic tale that had risen above time. She saw a youthful couple, deeply in love, however their bond had been unfortunately stopped by destiny.

In the twilight of a forbidden magical love, a girl and a boy, their hearts intertwined, found themselves ensnared in a tragic tale. Her family, blinded by prejudice, cast a shadow of mistrust upon the outsider who captured her heart. Love turned to turmoil, and in their anguish, they resorted to magic. Sparks flew, incantations whispered, and a dark enchantment was woven.

As the tempest raged, the girl's fragile form crumbled under the weight of their conflict, her life extinguished by the very magic meant to mend their love. Her essence, a spectral whisper, lingered in a precious gemstone, a silent testament to their ill-fated romance.

Their town, once a haven of harmony, became a battleground, with the divide between clans deepening. Bitter feuds ignited like wildfire, and the prospect of unity grew ever more distant, all while the girl's haunting presence continued to be heard, a sorrowful reminder of the love that was lost in the clutches of misunderstanding and magic.

Atop the desolate summit of Breaking Mountain, her earthly vessel found its final repose, nestled amidst the very heartbreak the mountain symbolized. As her last breath gently escaped her lips, she uttered an oath, echoed by her beloved.

"My cherished magical mountain, you alone bear witness to the shattered fragments of our love," she whispered with a heavy heart. "We vow that until the day our divided clans unite, this curse upon our souls shall remain unbroken."

Tears welled in her eyes as she told the vision to King Aryan. Together, they now understood that the mountain wept in sadness as well as in yearning for the love that had been lost. The Breaking Mountain was a sign of the power of love and the depths of its effect on the world.

With an undeterred determination, they carried on their mission on healing to the mountain and the town, they decided to host a fantastic festival of love. They welcomed couples from all over. Empowering them to restore their commitments and commend the affection that had endured for an extremely long period.

As the festival unfolded, the town woke up with giggling and happiness. Couples embraced and shared stories of their persevering through love. The air was filled not with distress anymore, but rather with the deep understanding that love was a power that could rise above even in the haziest of times.

Chenoa's eyes were aglow with wonder as she stood on the edge of a serene lakeside, surrounded by the majestic, snow-capped mountains. Her outstretched arm pointed gracefully at the breathtaking panorama before her. "Look," she whispered, her voice filled with awe, "how beautiful it is; it's full of grace and blessing."

The sun dipped below the horizon, casting a warm, golden hue over the landscape. The tranquil waters of the lake mirrored the sky's vibrant colors, creating a breathtaking reflection that seemed to unite heaven and earth in a harmonious embrace. The entire scene exuded a sense of serene magnificence.

Her father, a wise King Aryan, stood beside her, equally entranced by the view. With a smile that seemed to hold the wisdom of the ages, he nodded in agreement and said, "You are right, dear Chenoa. This is a sacred moment, a reminder of the divine beauty that surrounds us in the world. It is a testament to the grace and blessings that nature bestows upon us, a gift to cherish and protect."

Together, they stood in reverent silence, absorbing the profound beauty of the world around them. In that fleeting moment, the beauty of nature had not only enraptured their senses but also touched their souls, leaving an indelible mark on their hearts.

Amidst the breathtaking landscape of the mountain's heart, Chenoa's voice quivered with a sense of profound wonder. She exclaimed, "How magnificent it is, this is the mountain's heart. It no longer gives tears but happiness as the mountain gemstones have transformed into sparkling crystals, shining as bright as the sun." Her eyes glistened with gratitude, and she felt truly blessed to witness this transformation.

King Aryan, her father, stood beside her, his heart filled with pride and love. He gently replied, "Indeed, my daughter, it's as beautiful as your heart. Your compassion and determination have played a significant role in this wondrous change."

As they admired the radiant crystals glistening in the mountain's heart, they knew that the transformation was not only a testament to nature's resilience but also to the power of compassion and determination. Chenoa's heart was indeed as beautiful as the newfound splendor of the mountain, a symbol of the positive change one person could bring to the world.

As the moon ascended high over the Breaking Mountain, Princess Chenoa in her temporary dragon form and King Aryan remained at the summit of the mountain, witnessing a transformation before their eyes. The gemstones sparkled beautifully, no longer tears of sadness emanating out except for bittersweet tears delight, mirroring the love and bliss that had filled the town.

At that time of revelation, Chenoa figured out the true essence of her enchanted gifts. Love and empathy were not simply tools to break curses or heal wounds; they were actually the very essence of magic itself.

The power of love been able to change hearts as well as the world around them.

With the Breaking Mountain at peace, they bid goodbye to the town, realizing that their journey was nowhere over yet. Their quest had made into something far greater - a mission to spread love and kindness to every corner of the kingdom.

King Aryan sat alone, a single candle casting a warm, flickering light on the portraits adorning the walls. His eyes welled up with tears as he caressed a painting of his beloved Queen Leona. Memories of their time together flooded his mind, and he whispered softly, as though she were still with him, "My dear Leona, even though you've been gone for a long time, you remain alive in our memories. I've lost you, but I have our child, a living reminder of the love we shared. I promise to protect them just as you wish. It's time for me to accept that you are gone."

As he finished speaking, a gentle breeze rustled the curtains, as if a loving, invisible hand had reached out to comfort him. King Aryan knew that Leona's spirit would forever watch over their kingdom and their child, providing strength and guidance from the realms beyond. With newfound resolve, he stood up, wiping away his tears, determined to honor Leona's memory by being the best father he could be to their child and a wise ruler to his kingdom.

As they ventured forward, Princess Chenoa and King Aryan embraced the power of love in all forms. Their path turned into a celebration of the human heart, and they understood that their fate was to change the kingdom as well as to influence the world, one act of kindness at a time.

Thus, they strolled forward with hearts brimming with love, realizing that they were bound to make a world where kindness and peace ruled. Their journey had turned into a symbol of the magic of the heart, showing that love had the ability to change the existences of people as well as the destiny of a whole kingdom. Thus, they continued, joined in their motivation, prepared to embrace anything that what was in store held, realizing that the force of love would lead them towards a fate that was more superior than any curse or magic - a destiny woven with the strings of love and kindness, bound to impact the world.

In the stillness of the early morning, King Aryan stood alone on the balcony of his castle, the weight of his responsibilities and the memories of days long gone heavy on his heart. He gazed out across the kingdom, lost in his thoughts, when suddenly, a warm hand touched his back. Startled, he turned to find Chenoa, his daughter, standing there with a gentle smile on her face.

"My father," she said softly, "smile with your heart now. I understand what's in your heart. But we must let the past remain as memories. Instead, let us look to the future, for we are still here, living and breathing as humans. We must move forward to live and carry on our mother's love for eternity."

King Aryan felt a sense of comfort wash over him as he looked into his daughter's eyes, filled with both wisdom and compassion. Her words were a reminder that life was a continuous journey, and although they carried the weight of the past, they also had the gift of the present and the promise of the future.

As he smiled, he realized that the love and legacy of their mother would endure, carried forward by their shared determination to create a brighter and more hopeful tomorrow. It was a lesson in resilience and the enduring power of love, a reminder that in moving forward, they could honor their past and create a legacy that would span through eternity.

"Our mission is accomplished; now let's go to the next mission. Let's move forward." Chenoa said, smiling at her father.

Chapter 11: The Dancing Stars

"Oh, my shooting stars above,
Have you stolen away my scars with your celestial love?
If you have, I ask, please don't hesitate,
Keep them safe, but remember to compensate,
Return them to me, in exchange for my heart's artistry,
For it sparkles with a unique and wondrous beauty."

AS PRINCESS CHENOA and King Aryan traveled through the kingdom, their reputation as the conveyors of love and kindness grew. Their presence turned into an image of trust, and stories of their enchanted journeys arrived at the farthest corners of the realm.

One fateful evening, as they went under the heavenly canopy of stars, they coincidentally found a lively celebration occurring in a humble village. The Night of the Dancing Stars was a festival of unity and harmony, where people from various backgrounds and cultures met up to celebrate. Strangely, Princess Chenoa didn't turn a beast this time. She was in simply a normal human state.

Fascinated by the festivities, Princess Chenoa and her father also participated in the party, moving under the twinkling stars. Laughter and music filled the entire atmosphere of the night, and the joyous energy was contagious. They wondered about seeing individuals from assorted different backgrounds, dancing hand in hand, bound by the string of love and kindness.

In the center of the celebration, they met an older lady named Camilla, who was known for her magical wisdom and association with the stars. She looked at them with eyes that appeared to hold mysteries of the universe.

"Welcome, dear travelers," she said with a grin. "I sense the magic that encompasses you. Your journey has been honored by the universe."

Captivated by Camilla's words, Chenoa asked, "What do you mean, wise one? How is our journey associated with the stars?"

Her eyes twinkled with ancient knowledge. "The powers of fate have a way of aligning destinies in perfect orders," she said. "Your love and kindness have ignited a celestial dance, where the strings of destiny are intertwined. Your journey is important for a grand plan, guided by the very heavens above."

As they listened, they felt a feeling of awe and wonder, understanding that their journey was not just a simple journey. The stars had planned to unite them, and their actions had set in motion a divine dance of love and kindness, touching lives beyond their imagination.

"Now, as I stand here with the knowledge we've gleaned, it's clear that our path isn't merely a journey; it's a sacred odyssey toward a harmonious dream. This dream is not just an ephemeral reverie amongst the stars; it's a destination where we harmonize with the very universe, singing a celestial symphony of kindness." Chenoa said to them.

With appreciation in their hearts, they kept on moving under the stars, their steps guided by the rhythm of the universe. They understood that their main goal was not exclusively to heal the kingdom yet additionally to inspire others to embrace the force of love.

As the night came to dawn, Camilla offered them a divine gift. She raised her hands towards the night sky, and the stars appeared to shine with an ethereal glow. She whispered ancient oaths, causing the force of the universe to strengthen their magical powers.

"Combine your love and kindness into the structures of the world," Camilla said, her voice conveying the wisdom of ages. "The stars have picked you to become the guiding light in the darkest of times. Your path is carved in the skies, and your love will always enlighten the hearts of those you touch."

With Camilla's blessing, Princess Chenoa and King Aryan felt a flood of heavenly energy inside them. They understood that their journey was not just about breaking curses or spreading love in the kingdom; it was cosmic efforts that transcended both time and space.

"Goodbye now," they said, smiling gracefully at her.

As they bid goodbye to Camilla and The Night of the Dancing Stars, they realized that they were never again just explorers on a mission; they were heavenly dancers, guided by the stars above.

They wandered forward, prepared to embrace the fate that the stars had offered to them. They were joined by their love for one another as well as by the knowledge that they were important for a grand cosmic plan, where love and kindness were the guiding constellations.

Thus, Princess Chenoa and King Aryan ventured under the stars, their hearts laced with the divine rhythms, spreading love and kindness any place they went. Their steps had turned into a dance of stars, enlightening the world with their pure love, and thus, their fates were unchangingly interlaced with the boundless patterns of the universe.

"Embrace your essence, my cherished father. Together, we must fortify our resolve until the journey's end. As we tread the depths of the ocean floor, may we ascend to the heights of the starry skies. Our mission is a testament of compassion to all in order to adorn this world with the tapestry of peace, where war finds no place." Chenoa said, holding their hands together.

Chapter 12: The Tune of the Heart

"Will you lend an ear to me?
You are truly remarkable, you see,
This praise is not bestowed lightly,
For your magnificence shines brightly.
Now, listen to the melody within my heart's art,
Sung with all of me, a gift from my inner heart.
Kindness shall find its way to your door,
Never let your head hang low anymore,
Rise above, like a pearl on the ocean floor."

AS PRINCESS CHENOA and King Aryan proceeded with their celestial dance through the kingdom, their reputation as the carriers of love and kindness arrived at new levels. Their presence carried hope and healing to the hearts of all who crossed their way. People from far off lands went to witness the magic of their love and the extraordinary power of their kindness.

At some point, as they ventured through a bustling city, they met a gathering of street performers. Their melodic tunes swirled around, and the melodies talked about love, unity, and the magnificence of the human spirit. Drawn by the music, Princess Chenoa and King Aryan stopped to tune in, their hearts got enchanted by the beautiful songs.

"Father, take a look," Chenoa said while she pointed out to someone.

The lead performer, a singer named Enzo, saw the illustrious couple in the group and welcomed them to join the performance. With a grin, they took the performer's proposition, and together, they sang a melody of love and kindness and touched the spirits of everybody present.

As their voices orchestrated, a magical energy appeared to encompass them, and the very air hummed with celestial vibrations. Locals were moved to tears, feeling the love and compassion woven into each note. It was a melody of unity, rising above language and culture, binding the hearts of all who tuned in.

In the result of their impromptu performance, Enzo moved toward them, his eyes reflecting admiration and amazement. "Your love is a song that resonates with the universe," he said. "Your sympathy has the ability to heal even the deepest wounds."

Princess Chenoa and King Aryan gave thanks to Enzo for his thoughtful words, humbled by the impact their song had on individuals. They understood that their journey had turned into an orchestra of affection and empathy, touching lives and winding around an embroidery of unity and harmony.

"May you please let me join you?" Enzo asked, hoping that he could.

Enzo, inspired by their message, requested to go along with them on their journey. He felt a profound calling to be essential for their mission, spreading the magical of their adoration through his music. With open arms, Princess Chenoa and King Aryan invited Enzo into their team, thankful for the gift of his stirring songs.

"Join us, young man; let's embrace this world with peace and goodness," King Aryan said, opening his hand.

Enzo replied, his voice filled with conviction, "Yes, my King! I would stand by your side, and together, we shall make this world hear the sweet tune of peace." His words resonated with a passion for a better future, one where harmony and tranquility would reign over their realm.

The king, deeply moved by Enzo's commitment, nodded in agreement. "Then let us begin this noble journey together," he declared, "for it is our collective dedication that will bring about the change we seek. With unity and resolve, we shall compose the symphony of peace that will echo through the ages." Princess Chenoa smiled towards him, believing that this was their fate to accomplish their mission.

Together, they went all over, spreading their message of adoration and compassion through music. They performed in towns and towns, at grand festivals and humble social events. Every tune turned into a song of praise of trust, joining hearts and enclosing gaps.

Later, as they crossed the borders of the kingdom, they met a neighboring realm experiencing a harsh conflict. Two clans, once bound by friendship, were currently in dispute, destroyed by grudges.

The situation was critical, yet Princess Chenoa, King Aryan, and Enzo realized that their music had the ability to heal deepest wounds. They organized a fantastic show, welcoming people from the two clans to join in.

As the music started, an extraordinary magical energy consumed the space around them. The clans, at first guarded and far off, started to sway to the music, their hearts relaxed by the tunes of love and kindness. The rift that had isolated them for years started to patch, slowly.

Tears fell down on their cheeks, not tears of sadness, but rather tears of healing and reconciliation. Princess Chenoa, King Aryan, and Enzo saw that their music had gotten through the barriers of hatred, for it was a melody, yet a genuine expression of their unity and love for all.

The two clans embraced one another, tears blending in with smiles, and the kingdom just witness a miracle of transformation. The power of their music brought harmony to the fighting clans as well as ignited a light of trust in the hearts of all who were present.

As they bid goodbye to the unified realm, they realized that their journey had become more significant than ever. It was not just about breaking curses or spreading love in their own kingdom; it was tied in with encouraging unity and agreement across realms and borders.

Thus, they proceeded with their celestial dance, realizing that the song of their hearts would eternally resonate with the universe. Their journey had turned into a symphony of love and kindness, contacting lives and transforming the world each tune at a time. Hence, they strived forward, guided by the power of their music and the unwavering belief that love could heal even the deepest wounds and divided hearts.

"Brace yourself, young man, and let us keep lifting our spirits. This is our first mission with you being accomplished; congratulations; you have done well," Princess Chenoa said towards Enzo. Happy to him, so did King Aryan.

Chapter 13: The Gardens of Healing

"I assure you, kindness shall return to you,
Just gaze upon the captivating, sparkling hues,
Witness the aurora dancing in the skies so wide,
They're a testament, to your heart's gentle stride.
In the serene melody that plays its part,
These are your kind words, a gift from your heart."

PRINCESS CHENOA, KING Aryan, and Enzo continued with their adventure. Their belief as the bearers of love and understanding which had now grown further and wide. News about their celestial dance and soul-blending music had touched the hearts of countless souls, and people from multiple different backgrounds sought for their guidance and comfort.

One day, they got a request from a neighboring kingdom nearby known for its beautiful gardens. The kingdom's King, Queen Maeve, had heard about their magical journey and the transformative force of their love. She yearned to meet them, hoping that their presence could bring healing to her own kingdom, which was experiencing a mysterious disease that had befallen its gardens.

Interested by the request, they advanced toward the kingdom of rich gardens. However, upon arrival, they were met with a sight that left them dull. The once beautiful gardens were now withered and abandoned, their colors blurred and their elegance defaced by a strange darkness.

Queen Maeve welcomed them with a heavy heart, her eyes reflecting the sadness that had befallen upon her kingdom. She explained to them that regardless of their endeavors from the kingdom's best gardeners and mages, the gardeners remained tormented by a curse that appeared to be unbreakable.

Still, Princess Chenoa and her companions set off on a mission to investigate the gardens, looking for the source of the curse. As they wandered through the maze of paths, they could sense the presence of an ancient, dark and unmoving magic.

In the core of the gardens, they found an old chair covered in ivy and moss. The chair radiated an aura of sorrow and despair. Intrigued, Princess Chenoa moved toward the well and touched its weathered stones, feeling a surge of distress from deep within.

Through her enchanted gifts, she was able to access a dream from the past, seeing the story of a taboo love that had led to catastrophe and suffering. The curse was born into the world from the pain of lost love, and its coils had saturated deep into the gardens.

In a realm beset by a magical war, a once-mighty king faced a dire loss—the impending departure of his beloved queen. She had always been the enchantress on the throne, weaving spells and enchantments with her every grace. Their garden, a haven of both joy and sorrow, bore witness to her every incantation. But when she fell victim to the cruel forces of the war, the king's world crumbled.

He stood before the throne, their last meeting place, and with tears in his eyes, he whispered," My dearest queen, as you depart, it's not just my heart that is lost, but all that I cherish in this realm will soon fade into oblivion."

With newly discovered understanding, Princess Chenoa projected out the vision to her partners and Queen Maeve. She instantly understood that the only way to break the curse was not in overcoming a dark power but rather in healing the hearts troubled by sorrow and resentment.

With compassion and wisdom, they assembled individuals of the kingdom, empowering them to share their stories of loss and agony. As people opened their hearts, they released the repressed feelings that had fueled the curse.

"Put your mind into your heart; your heart will listen to those voices with the power of your heart; let yourself be free from that sadness; fill it with your happiness. Listen to it...listen." Princess Chenoa said to them: To the person who held grudges, sadness, and despairs for a long time.

"It's time. Let it pass..." Princess Chenoa said again to them. With her voices, she was trying to soothe them, hoping they would be free from any resentments.

In the center of the gardens, a change began to unfold. The wilted plants started to sprout again, and vibrant colors returned to their original beautiful forms. The power of love and sympathy had brought out a light of trust that spread like wildfire, carrying new life to the land.

Princess Chenoa, King Aryan, and Enzo realized that their main goal which was to break curses as well as to heal the injuries that lay deep inside each soul. The gardens had turned into a symbol of resilience and renewal, a testament of the force of love to bring life even despite darkness.

As they bid farewell to Queen Maeve and her kingdom, again, they realized that their adventure had taken on another important step further. Their journey was tied in with spreading love and kindness as well as about healing the broken hearts of all they touched.

Therefore, they continued again with their celestial dance with the guidance of the stars. They also knew that the force of their love was not restricted by time or space. Their journey had turned into a symphony of healing, transforming the world into a better place. Thus, they ventured yet again forward, steered by the knowledge that love not only could heal even the most broken souls but also restore the beauty of the world, one garden each in turn.

Chapter 14: The Bewitched Waters

"In the tranquil land and by the gentle river's side,
Amidst the melodious water's soothing tide,
I discern your voice, a whisper in the breeze,
Speaking to my soul, putting my heart at ease.
I listen closely, and I hear you say,
'Kindness shall return, come what may.'
It shall weave its path, like the wandering wind so true,
Returning to you, with victories anew."

AS PRINCESS CHENOA, King Aryan, and Enzo traveled on their journey, their way driven them to a mysterious domain known for its magical waters. The kingdom of flowing streams and gleaming lakes was said to hold mysterious powers, capable of uncovering one's actual desires and fears.

Charmed by the legends encompassing the kingdom's waters, they moved toward the shore of the Great Lake of Dreams. Its surface resembled liquid crystal, mirroring the moon's gentle glow, and a feeling of serenity wrapped them.

Guided by an internal calling, Princess Chenoa dunked her hand into the water, and the surface woke up with a soft sparkle. The lake appeared to sense the pureness of her heart, and again, a dream appeared before her eyes.

In that dream, she saw a young man standing by the shore, his eyes filled with bitterness. The man couldn't talk, troubled by an old curse that had taken his voice. He yearned in vain more than to seek his true voice and be liberated from the charm that silenced him.

Princess Chenoa then imparted the vision to King Aryan and Enzo, and they realized that it's time for another mission. They knew they came there for a reason. So, they set off on a mission to find the man, realizing that their journey was tied in with breaking curses as well as about granting the most profound longings of the heart.

After a while of looking, they at long last tracked down the man, named Shua, concealed in a hidden cave. His eyes widened with surprise as they drew nearer, and he appeared to sense their main intention to help him with finding his real voice.

"It's you, you are the one who came into my dream last night, right?" she asked to Shua.

Shua just smiled to them.

"I came, my friend, we will help you to get this through," Princess Chenoa determined to help him out.

With a delicate touch, Princess Chenoa utilized her enchanted gifts, and suddenly a silver light encompassed Shua. A magical melody consumed the space, and incredibly, Shua's voice started to come out. It was soft at first, however it grew louder as time passed, breaking the silence that had caught him for such a long time.

Tears of joy spilled down Shua's cheeks as he spoke the first time in many years, his voice filled with appreciation and wonder. He shared his story, how an old curse had taken his ability to speak as a youngster, leaving him trapped in silence and isolation.

Moved by Shua's newly found voice, Princess Chenoa, King Aryan, and Enzo understood that their mission was not just about breaking condemnations or recuperating wounds but also granting the deepest desires of those they met.

With Shua's voice recovered, they traveled to the core of the Great Lake of Dreams, where ancient waters held the power to uncover one's deepest longings and fears. They chose to face the mysterious waters although knowing that their disclosures might be both enlightening and challenging.

"Dear Princess, thank you for healing me. Now take this with you. You already passed these trials; however, more are yet to come. Embrace yourself, never keep your head down, look for the skies; you will find your way soon. That's the first and last piece of advice that Shua gave her. She would keep remembering it. Shua was giving her a silver and gold bracelet attached to pure water from that magical water. It was blue, and now it has turned white, pure as a cloud. Princess Chenoa didn't know what would happen, but she believed it had something special about it.

As they ventured into the waters, dreams projected before their eyes - desires they had long kept hidden, fears that had lurked in the deepest of their souls. The captivated waters encouraged them to face these truths, to embrace their weaknesses, and to seek the strength in their unity.

At that time, they comprehended that their journey had turned into a reflection of the human spirit - a sewing woven with love, kindness, healing, and the revelation of one's true self.

As they emerged from the Great Lake of Dreams, a newfound discovered feeling of purpose filled in their hearts. They found out that they had another purpose which was guiding others to confront their deepest desires and fears.

They proceeded with their heavenly dance, realizing that the force of their affection and sympathy was boundless. Their travels had turned into an ensemble of self-discovery, and they embraced the knowledge that by helping other people to face their own deepest desires and fears.

Thus, they wandered forward with a new revelation by the magical waters and the disclosure that their mission was tied in with transforming the world as well as about evolving themselves, slowly and carefully. Their journey had turned into a song of the heart, a dance of transformation, and they embraced the destinies that awaited for them with open hearts and unwavering love.

With unwavering determination, she spoke, "One day, the world will witness that our journey is as pure as the crystal waters and as unyielding as the mighty sea. Just gaze upon the ocean; it forever seeks the embrace of the shore. In the same way, our dream will find its path to fruition, and someday, it will be a tangible reality."

Chapter 15: The Maze of Mirrors

"In these trials, within life's intricate maze,
I've discovered you, my constant race.
I've run and run, yet couldn't quite ace,
But now I've learned, in this heart's grace,
To pause, to savor, and truly embrace,
The beauty of the journey, in life's endless chase."

PRINCESS CHENOA, KING Aryan, and Enzo's celestial dance led them to the edges of a mysterious timberland known as the Maze of Mirrors. The forest was said to hold illusions that could uncover the deepest truths and secrets of one's soul. Intrigued by the test that lay ahead, they entered the maze with courage and determination.

As they wandered further into the maze, they were met with a kaleidoscope of reflections, each mirror showing various parts of themselves. A few mirrors uncovered moments of unity and kindness, while others reflected uncertainty and weakness.

In the middle of the maze, they found an enormous mirror that appeared to hold a powerful magic. As they moved toward it, the mirror sparkled, and their appearance transformed into different versions of themselves -versions that conveyed the heaviness of their previous mistakes and regrets.

Her father, puzzled, inquired, "What is this sensation? It feels so peculiar."

Enzo replied, "Indeed, our King, it chills us to the bone and sends shivers down our spines."

With wisdom in her voice, the King's daughter, Chenoa, spoke gently, "Let us embrace the memories of our past, my dear father and friend. This sensation seems to beckon us, to draw our attention to it. But we shall learn from it, and in the face of sadness, we shall find the strength to reflect and move forward."

Suddenly, the magical mirror, dormant for so long, began to tremble, as if resonating with her words, its surface quivering as if awakened by the echoes of their shared resolve.

Chenoa saw her reflection encompassed in the shadows of self-doubt, tormented by memories of times when her love and kindness had wavered. King Aryan saw his reflection troubled by the weight of obligations as a King, battling to adjust his obligation and his longing for a peaceful kingdom. Enzo saw his reflection overwhelmed in the echoes of past disappointments, feeling unworthy of the job he played in their adventure.

Amidst this emotional revelation, they comprehended that their journey was not just about breaking curses and spreading love. It was facing their inner demons and finding strength in their weaknesses.

With a collective breath, they closed their eyes, each one determined to confront their vulnerabilities. Chenoa, a beacon of strength, encouraged them, saying, "Hold on tight."

Their hands joined in unity, forming a circle of shared resolve. Chenoa, the enchantress of the moment, began to weave her words into a heartfelt incantation.

"Dear weaknesses within us, I acknowledge your enduring presence in the corridors of our memories. But now, as we journey forward into our future, let us part ways. May you be touched by the warmth of our kindness and the brilliance of our goodness, allowing your wounds to be mended, and your darkness to be lifted."

With recently discovered clarity, they reached out to each other, supporting each other as they faced their dark reflections. The maze seemed to recognize their willingness to embrace their imperfections, and the mirrors transformed into ethereal mists, dissipating into the air.

A voice echoed through the maze, gently. "You have come to comprehend that genuine strength lies in embracing your flaws and learning from the past," the voice said. "Simply by recognizing your own shadows, you can harness the full force of your light."

As they went on through the maze, they encountered mirrors that showed their difficulties as well as their victories and resilience. They saw moments when their love and kindness had touched many lives, and how their unity had ignited trust in the hearts of others.

The mirrors reflected the profound effect their journey had on the world, painting a tapestry of interconnected souls united by affection and understanding. They understood that their mission had turned into a testament of the power of the human soul to transcend difficulty and embrace the beauty of imperfections.

At the core of the maze, they found a last mirror that mirrored their unified selves. Their souls entwined with the celestial dance of love and kindness. It was a reflection of their adventure, a reminder that their fates were eternally bound by the strings of destiny and love.

Eventually, they came out from the Maze of Mirrors, they felt a significant identity acknowledgment and solidarity. Their process had developed into a more profound investigation of their own spirits and the spirits of those they contacted on the way.

Inseparably, they proceeded with their divine dance, realizing that the power of their love and kindness extended beyond the limits of the kingdom and into the hearts of all they experienced. Their journey had turned into an orchestra of self-revelation, and they embraced the predetermination that looked for them with open hearts and immovable love.

Thus, they traveled forward, guided by the illustrations of the maze and the disclosure that their mission was tied in with impacting the world as well as about changing themselves, slowly. Their journey had turned into a dance of transformation, a journey of mirrors that reflected the beauty of their souls and the boundless potential of love and kindness.

In the quiet of her solitude, she wore a serene smile, a graceful curve of contentment. With a voice like a gentle breeze, she whispered, "Dear past, may you now find your place among the bygones, rest peacefully, and trouble us no more."

As her words dispersed into the air, the weight of yesterday seemed to lift, leaving behind a sense of tranquility and newfound hope. It was a moment of closure, a turning point in her journey toward a brighter and unburdened future.

Chapter 16: The Sanctuary of Whispers

"The gentle sound of the windflowers,
I lend my ear to their soft, melodious powers.
They whisper secrets, so tender and smart,
Directly to my heart, where they find their start."

AS PRINCESS CHENOA, King Aryan, and Enzo proceeded with their celestial dance, their journey led them to a secret sanctuary settled nestled inside a lavish valley. The Sanctuary of Whispers was a place of ancient knowledge, where the breezes conveyed the voices of the past and the secrets of the universe.

Drawn by the asylum's magical aura, they entered its holy grounds with admiration. A silent tranquility wrapped them as they ventured into the core of the safe-haven, where an old tree stood tall and magnificent, its branches coming to towards the sky.

At the base of the tree, they found an old woman sitting in reflection. Her eyes, the shade of wisdom, shimmered with a knowing sparkle. She welcomed them with a comforting smile, recognizing the importance of their arrival.

"You have come looking for answers, youthful wanderers," the old woman said, her voice a delicate murmur that appeared to resonate with the breezes. "The Sanctuary of Whispers holds the wisdom of ages, and the mysteries of the universe are whispered in its embrace."

Princess Chenoa, King Aryan, and Enzo humbly communicated their desire to understand the deeper meaning of their journey. They sought to understand the links of their quests and the reason that had joined them in this celestial dance.

The old woman welcomed them to sit underneath the old tree, where the gentle rustling of leaves seemed to convey the melody of the universe. She explained that their journey had risen above the limits of a simple mission; it had turned into an embroidery woven by the actual universe, guided by the strings of adoration and empathy.

"As you touched the existences of others, you became agent for change," the old woman said, his words conveying the heaviness of ancient knowledge. "Your love and kindness have awakened the dormant seeds of hope in the hearts of many, and your celestial dance has set in motion a symphony of transformation."

She discussed how their journey had turned into a reflection of the human soul's ability for growth and strength. Each challenge they faced, every heart they touched, and each soul they healed had turned into a piece of the greater symphony of existence.

Princess Chenoa, King Aryan, and Enzo listened with careful attention, absorbing the significant wisdom that the sanctuary advertised. The old woman encouraged them to trust in the guidance of their hearts and the power of their love, for they were not only wanderers on a mission; they were problem solvers in a universe that longed for healing and unity.

With recently discovered information and a profound feeling of purpose, they said thanks to the sage for her wisdom and blessings. As they arranged to leave the sanctuary, the old tree appeared to whisper words of encouragement, helping them to remember their connection with every single living being and the unlimited capability of their love.

Enzo, his eyes gleaming with determination, stood beside them, ready to embark on the journey of their dreams. With unwavering resolve, he declared, "I will stand by your side, my dear King and Princess. Together, we will set sail on the seas of goodness, and our united hearts will guide us through this magnificent adventure." Their shared commitment was the beginning of a remarkable tale where friendship, courage, and unity would shape their destiny.

As they continued their celestial dance, realizing that the force of their affection and sympathy reached out beyond the boundaries of their kingdom. Their quest had turned into an orchestra of spirits, each note addressing the extraordinary effect of their actions on the lives they contacted.

Her father's eyes sparkled with warmth as he smiled at her. "We will do this together, my dear daughter," he assured, his voice filled with unwavering support. "I will be there to help you with Enzo. Together, we will sing this kindness to the world. Never allow your weaknesses to embrace you; instead, let your kind heart touch the world. Let our kindness be the beacon of light in the darkest of times." Their bond was a promise of love and unity, a melody of hope and compassion that would resonate far and wide.

Again, they continued forward with the guidance of the wisdom of the sanctuary as well as by the acknowledgment that their journey was tied in with impacting the world as well as about growing themselves slowly. Their journey had turned into a dance of transformation, an journey of whispers that echoed through the universe, setting off the fire of hope and love in every heart they touched.

"I swear to myself," she whispered, her voice a gentle breeze. "This kindness will remain forever in this whole universe, an eternal flame that no darkness can extinguish. It will shine brighter than any star, illuminating the skies, the moon, and the hearts of mankind." With her hands clasped in prayer, she made a solemn vow to the cosmos.

Chapter 17: The Divine Revelation

"To the moon and stars above, I adore your grace,
Can you hear my voice, in this tranquil space?
I sing a lullaby, so beautiful and sweet,
Come, embrace me now, in your soothing retreat,
Wrap me in serenity, let my worries cease,
In your radiant presence, may I find inner peace."

AS THE DIVINE JOURNEY of Princess Chenoa, King Aryan, and Enzo continued, their journey drove them to a sacred mountaintop, bathed in the glow of a thousand stars. The air was touched with expectation, for it was said that the mountain top held the way to opening the secrets of the universe.

Directed by their instinct, they climbed the mountaintop with awe in their hearts. At the summit, a radiant beam of light encompassed them, lifting them to a higher plane of consciousness. They found themselves surrounded by celestial creatures, their luminous presence enlightening the evening.

One of the celestial creatures stepped forward, her eyes shining with heavenly wisdom. "Welcome, brave souls," she welcomed them in a pleasant voice. "You have ventured so far, guided by the celestial dance of affection and sympathy. Presently, you stand at the limit of a profound revelation."

Princess Chenoa, King Aryan, and Enzo listened eagerly. Their spirits were opened to the wisdom that awaited them. The celestial explained that their journey had not been a simple series of journeys yet a heavenly ensembled and coordinated by the universe.

"You are messengers of affection and empathy," the divine being revealed. "Your unified souls have woven an embroidery of interconnectedness, transcending time and space. The power of your love has touched lives beyond your kingdom, kindling off the fire of trust in the hearts of many souls."

She further discussed how their divine dance had ignited a flood of change, setting in a chain response of affection that resounded through the universe. Their journey had turned into a heavenly revelation, a demonstration of the boundless capability of the human heart when motivated by love and unity.

As the celestial spoke, memories of their experiences overwhelmed their minds - the cursed souls they had mended, the kingdoms they had joined together, and the hearts they had contacted. They understood that their journey had not only been tied in with breaking curses yet about awakening the dormant seeds of adoration and empathy inside each soul they encountered.

"You are the conveyors of a cosmic symphony," the celestial being said. "Your adoration and empathy have blended the universe, joining souls and galaxies in a dance of divine love."

With a feeling of direction and appreciation, they embraced the disclosure. They comprehended that their quest was not even close to finished, for the orchestra of affection and sympathy would everlastingly play on, directing them towards new horizons and unknown destinies.

As they descended from the peak, the heavenly creatures offered to them a gift - a divine song that would everlastingly reverberate in their souls. It was an indication of their sacred mission, a dance that rose above the limits of reality.

They continued their divine dance, realizing that their mission had turned into a heavenly revelation, an orchestra of adoration and sympathy that would resonate until the end of time. They comprehended that their adventure was linked with transforming the world as well as about changing the universe, each note of affection in turn.

Thus, they carried on their steps forward, directed by the insight of the divine revelation and the information that their mission was connected with changing themselves as well as about changing the universe. Their journey had turned into a heavenly dance of unity and love, and they embraced the fate that awaited them with open hearts and unwavering devotion.

Under the open sky, with the earth as their witness, they raised their voices in a harmonious song, a solemn oath to the cosmos.

"Dear sky and earth, hear our heartfelt plea. May peace reside in our minds and hearts, and from there, let it radiate across this vast universe, reaching those in need. Universe, grant us the strength to ease the burdens of our dear people." Their voices carried their hopes and aspirations, echoing through the cosmos.

Chapter 18: The Unearthly Friendliness

"My entire universe, a breathtaking display,
My ability to dance with grace, I pray,
May it shatter the chains, in a radiant ballet,
Replacing darkness with the kindness of day."

AS PRINCESS CHENOA, King Aryan, and Enzo followed their heavenly dance, they found themselves attracted to a gleaming waterfall deep inside a magical forest. The waterfall's flowing waters appeared to emit an entrancing song, and the air was filled with an ethereal harmony.

Captivated by the charming appeal of the cascade, they moved toward its glasslike pool. As they dunked their hands into the water, they felt a flood of energy, a harmonious resonance that connected them to the essence of the universe.

Out of nowhere, a gathering of ethereal creatures rose up out of the flowing waters, their forms radiant with divine light. They presented themselves as the Guardians of Harmony, watchmen of the cosmic balance.

"We have been anticipating your appearance," the Guardians spoke in a unified voice that echoed like the breeze. "Your divine dance has stirred the cosmic energies, and your journey has turned into a symphony of love and compassion that has touched the fabric of the universe."

Princess Chenoa, King Aryan, and Enzo were full in awe, humbled by the acknowledgment that their mission had far-reaching outcomes beyond anything they could ever imagine.

The Guardians revealed that their quest was not just about breaking curses or spreading love; it was also tied in with restoring the balance of the universe. They explained that the universe flourished with harmony, and each demonstration of adoration and sympathy reverberated with the celestial symphony, making waves of healing and unity.

"We are the watchmen of cosmic balance," the Guardians said. "In the ethereal harmony of the universe, each soul plays a unique note, and together, they form a heavenly melody that sustains the universe."

They told how the symphony of love and kindness had carried light to the haziest corners of existence, recovering the injuries of the past and igniting hope in the hearts of the miserable ones.

Moved by the significant truth, Princess Chenoa, King Aryan, and Enzo comprehended that their heavenly dance was a progression of journeys as well as a sacred mission to co-make with the universe.

As they washed in the ethereal waters, they embraced the cosmic harmony inside their souls, realizing that they were nevertheless instruments in the amazing orchestra of existence. The Guardians gave to them a gift - a heavenly melody that would eternally resonate inside their souls, helping them to remember their interconnectedness with the universe.

As Princess Chenoa stood on the brink of her transformation into a fearsome dragon creature, her eyes filled with despair. But in that moment, the heavens responded to her unspoken plea. The stars began to twinkle and sing a celestial lullaby, their melodies dancing across the night sky.

In the soothing chorus of the stars, a comforting message resonated:

"To our beloved humankind, dear princess, may your curse pass and be missed. Your trials are finally at an end. Let your heart, so magical and kind, become a beacon of power and kindness, lighting the way for all."

As the starlight surrounded her, Princess Chenoa felt the curse lift and her heart fill with newfound strength. She was destined to be a force of benevolence; her magical heart is now a source of hope and love for her people.

Princess Chenoa's heart overflowed with joy as she realized that her long-standing curse had been broken. Tears of happiness welled up in her eyes as King Aryan rushed to her, embracing his daughter with profound love.

With a quiver in his voice and tears glistening in his eyes, King Aryan whispered, "You did it, my dear daughter; now you will be free."

Enzo, standing nearby, couldn't contain his happiness. His applause rang out through the courtyard, celebrating not only the end of the curse but the beautiful bond between father and daughter. Enzo's heart swelled with happiness as he witnessed the culmination of their arduous journey and the triumph of love over adversity. The trials were over, and the warmth of family and friendship filled the air, bringing an end to a long and challenging chapter in their lives.

Inseparably, they continued their heavenly dance, realizing that their journey had turned into a vast ensemble, a dance of congruity and solidarity that reverberated through the universe. They understood that their process was tied in with impacting the world as well as about orchestrating with the grandiose energies that moved through every living being.

Thus, they wandered forward, guided by an additional insight of the Guardians and the information that their journey was bound with changing themselves as well as about becoming one with the ethereal harmony of the universe. Their process had turned into a heavenly dance of unity and love, and they embraced the fate that looked for them with open hearts and a significant feeling of vast reason.

Chapter 19: The Cosmic Bond

"This world can be a place of breathtaking beauty,
When people choose to be kind, their hearts in unity.
Imagine the splendor, imagine the serene,
Is it possible, you ask? Yes, in kindness, we glean."

AS PRINCESS CHENOA, King Aryan, and Enzo moved forward with their divine dance, their hearts were filled with the wisdom of the Guardians of Harmony. Their mission was connected with impacting the world as well as about adjusting their souls to the cosmic energies that coursed through every living being.

Guided by the heavenly melody inside their souls, they left on the last period of their excursion. Their way driven them to a secret hut placed on a mountain ridge, where the stars appeared to sparkle brightly.

At the entry of the hut, they were welcomed by an old lady, her eyes mirroring the eternal wisdom of the universe. She invited them with a soft smile and talked in a voice that resounded like the echoes of time eternity.

"Princess Chenoa, King Aryan, and Enzo, you have ventured all over, touched countless spirits, and harmonized with the cosmic symphony," the old lady said. "The opportunity has arrived for your cosmic union, the converging of your celestial souls with the essence of the universe."

As they ventured into the small cave behind the hut, they suddenly sensed a flood of vast energy surrounding them. The cave was decorated with divine images, each addressing a novel part of the enormous dance they had exemplified all through their journey.

In the core of the cave, a shining heavenly portal was opened as if was waiting for their arrival. The portal appeared to swell with energy, a passage to the vast universe.

The old lady told them that their cosmic union was not only a converging of souls; it was a divine of greatness, an acknowledgment that they were interconnected with each living being and heavenly entity in the universe.

"With each act of affection and sympathy, you have woven strings of light into the cosmic embroidery," she said. "Your celestial dance has set in motion an ensemble of unity, and presently, you will become one with the very essence of the universe."

Thus, they moved toward the gateway, their hearts open to the infinite energies that allured them. As they ventured through the portal, a splendid light encompassed them, and they felt a significant feeling of unity, a bond with the universe.

In that cosmic moment, they comprehended that their mission had driven them to a more profound truth - that adoration and sympathy were feelings as well as the essence of existence itself. They were humans on a journey as well as vast creatures moving in harmony like dancing as one with the universe.

As they arose out of the heavenly entrance, their souls aglow with divine light, they felt the presence of the Guardians of Harmony and the old lady, the echoes of their wisdom resonating within their beings.

Amidst a serene meadow bathed in the soft glow of twilight, Princess Chenoa extended her hand, her eyes filled with warmth and compassion. She said to those gathered around her, "Take my hand!" With unwavering trust, they clasped hands, forming a circle that seemed to shimmer with magic and purpose.

Chenoa's voice, filled with grace and intent, resonated through the gathering. "My people, moon, and stars, my whole universe," she began, her words carrying a weight of deep conviction. "Let us be as one, bound by kindness, goodness, and compassion. Spread these virtues all around the world like a radiant beacon of hope. Together, let us be a united force, harmonious and unwavering."

As her words hung in the air, a sense of unity and purpose enveloped the assembly. They felt connected not only to one another but to the very essence of the world and the universe above. Chenoa's enchantment had created a profound bond, one that would guide them in their mission to share kindness and harmony with the world, a reminder that unity and compassion were the keys to a brighter future.

Inseparably, they looked out into the tremendous region of the universe, their hearts filled with love and gratitude. They realized that their journey had turned into an enormous dance, a dance of unity and harmony that transcended time and space.

Again, they wandered forward, guided by the infinite energies that flowed through their souls and the wisdom that their journey was tied in with changing themselves as well as about becoming one with the true essence of the universe. Their quest had turned into a divine dance of unity and love, and they embraced the fate that awaited them with open hearts and a significant feeling of cosmic purpose.

Their celestial dance kept, weaving strings of adoration and empathy into the embroidery of the universe, an ensemble that echoed until the end of time, setting off the fire of hope and love in each heart they experienced. They found that their mission had turned into a dance of cosmic significance, a dance that harmonized with the universe, a dance of everlasting affection. Thus, they moved on, their souls eternally joined in the celestial embrace of the universe.

In a world that had long been marred by conflict, Princess Chenoa, her father, King Aryan, and their trusted advisor Enzo had tirelessly worked to foster peace and unity among their people and the animals that roamed their lands. After many years of dedication, they stood on a hill, overlooking a realm that had undergone a remarkable transformation.

The once turbulent and divided kingdom had become a haven of harmony. People from all walks of life, as well as the creatures that shared their world, now coexist peacefully. The echo of hatred, the shadow of conflict, and the stain of bloody battles were no more. They had united as one, a diverse tapestry of compassion and understanding.

Chenoa, her heart filled with gratitude and joy, turned to her father and Enzo. With a radiant smile, she said, "Finally, our mission has reached the hearts of people across the world. May we always be blessed with this harmonious world, where unity and compassion reign supreme." Her words were a testament to the extraordinary journey they had undertaken, the challenges they had faced, and the lasting legacy of peace they had created.

King Aryan and Enzo nodded in agreement, knowing that the effort they had put into creating this better world had been worthwhile. It was a world where the sounds of laughter and the colors of love now painted the landscape and where peace and unity were the guiding principles. As they stood together, the kingdom's newfound harmony was not just a testament to their efforts but a symbol of what could be achieved when people worked together for the greater good.

Chapter 20: The Eternal Legacy

"O, dear land of magical hope,
May your soul awaken and elope,
Rise from the depths of the ocean's scope,
Emerging like a wondrous miracle, full of hope."

PRINCESS CHENOA, KING Aryan, and Enzo's divine dance carried on, and with each step, they felt the endless energies of the universe coursing through their beings. As they journeyed together, their presence touched hearts and gave warm affection and sympathy any place they went.

The kingdom they once called home presently flourished in a harmonious symphony of unity, guided by the insight and love that the royal trio had imparted. The people, once divided by curses and conflicts, presently stood united, embracing the groundbreaking power of love.

The tradition of their cosmic union was carved into the hearts of all who had been moved by their divine dance. Songs and stories of their compassion and courage spread all over far and wide, inspiring generations to come.

In the years that followed, the kingdom bloomed into a haven of love and understanding, setting an example for neighboring lands to follow. The celestial dance had left an everlasting legacy, and the tapestry of their journey continued to weave threads of hope and change all through the world.

As they wandered past their kingdom's lines, their love and kindness reverberated with their lands, making a worldwide development of unity and harmony. Their quest had turned into a celestial ripple, spreading the illumination of understanding and acknowledgment to the farthest corners of the world.

They experienced kingdoms tormented by darkness and misery, offering a guiding hand and healing touch. Through their celestial dance, they showed that kindness knew no limits, and the force of love rose above all obstacles.

Together, they established schools of wisdom and compassion, where the teachings of the cosmic symphony were passed down to people in the future. The world embraced their inheritance, and the wisdom of their process turned into a guiding light for all searchers of truth and love.

Yet again the heavenly creatures and an old lady showed up, their eyes filled with adoration for the trio's celestial dance. They realized that this moment marked the satisfaction of a cosmic prophecy, the perfection of a long journey that had changed the world as well as the whole universe.

As they entered into the heavenly gateway one final time, their souls converged with the essence of the universe, turning into a divine orchestra of love and kindness. Their dance reverberated until the end of time, an immortal song that resounded in each side of the universe.

Thus, Princess Chenoa, King Aryan, and Enzo's divine dance continued, their adoration and empathy forever interweaved with the cosmic energies. Their legacy lived on, their souls perpetually directing the hearts of the people who looked for love and unity in the celestial dance of life.

One day, Enzo was reuniting with his childhood friend, Dahlia. She was the only one who was patiently waiting for him to come back for his world mission with them. They were tying the knots. Princess Chenoa and King Aryan were happy and sent their blessings by attending their wedding. It's a mesmerizing wedding. Far from the side, someone was watching Princess Chenoa.

During the dancing floor, Princess Chenoa was being invited by one young man.

"Dear Princess, will you dance with me?" he asked. Princess Chenoa smiled and then accepted his invitation.

They were dancing gracefully, and King Aryan was watching them, adoring them.

After dancing, that man with the mask was giving something to her.

It's a small cloth with a mystery flag trademark on it. Princess Chenoa wondered and asked him, "Wait, who are you? What is it?

He smiled and walked away without giving answers.

That night, Princess Chenoa was looking at the small cloth that was given to her by him that day. She was looking at it attentively. All of the sudden, her silver and gold bracelet fell from her wrist. She took it and wiped it off with the small cloth. Then something magical happened. The silver and gold bracelet, which Shua gave as a present, it was attached to Maya's gemstone. It was shaking slowly.

There was blue shining coming from the bracelet and spreading towards the floor, then across the town all of a sudden. It was happening fast.

All people were mesmerized by the land turned into a magical kingdom. The flowers were flying around with their sparkling magic, and the land turned bright. The tree and its leaves were moving around as it was dancing. The miraculous sound was singing. It's been a peaceful night.

With all of the help and passion they had shown, Finally, it awakened the bracelet that Shua's gave her during her journey. It turned into a gemstone. Same with the gemstone that King Aryan had before. That night, their kingdom turned back into a magical land of hope, Ankaa.

Princess Chenoa was shocked at first, and King Aryan then smiled proudly. Their tears were coming down. They were hugging each other. Now the gemstone has come back with its power. Thus, their kingdom will be the strongest power in this world.

As time passed, their physical forms aged, however their souls remained everlastingly young, laced with the everlasting dance of the universe. Their affection for one another developed further as time passes, an affection that exceeded all rational limitations and defied the constraints of time and space.

In the twilight of their lives, as they got back to the holy temple at the mountain ridge, they realized that their celestial dance was arriving at its climax. Encircled by the radiant energy of the universe, they held each other's hands, their hearts overflowing with appreciation and satisfaction.

Chapter 21: Delightful Promise

"Promise to hold onto this kindness within,
In its embrace, the world shall mend,
Gradually, we'll forge a path to heaven,
Where all is well, and love will resonate."

AFTER MANY ADVENTURES and a journey that rose above the limits of existence, Princess Chenoa found her love in the neighboring country, Kingdom of Eden. She was married to a King Noah, known for his handsome features and kind-hearted nature. The wedding ceremony was a great festival, an association of hearts and kingdoms, where love and sympathy were the guiding stars.

With the favors of the universe and the love for her husband, Princess Chenoa's transformation into a monster was nevertheless ancient history. A past. A distant memory. The curse had been broken, and her heart now soared with joy and contentment.

Her father, the King who had been close by all through their divine dance, remained by her during the wedding, glad and cheerful to observe his daughter's joy. The connection between them had developed further through their journey, and they valued the memories of their extraordinary mission.

Within the presence of their families, companions, and the heavenly creatures they had experienced, the wedding was a demonstration of the power of love and kindness in changing individual lives as well as whole kingdoms. The divine orchestra of their adventure resonated through the celebrations, helping all present to remember the astronomical meaning of their union.

As the days transformed into many weeks into months, Princess Chenoa and her spouse's adoration for one another grew. Their marriage was an encouraging sign and unity, bridging the gap between their kingdoms and cultivating a bond of understanding and respect.

The previous three faithful companions who had once accompanied with Princess Chenoa on her journey were currently her most trusted colleagues in the castle. Through her acts of kindness, they had been changed from a deer, a hare, and a sparrow into human forms. They were ever thankful for her sympathy and committed their lives to serving and safeguarding her.

Kingdom of Ankaa and Kingdom of Zvevda were flourished under the kindhearted rule of Princess Chenoa and her husband, King Noah. Their adoration and sympathy touched the hearts of people, moving them to embrace unity and turn out together for everyone's mutual understanding and respect.

The tradition of their celestial dance lived on in the hearts of all who knew their story. Songs and stories of their quest were passed down through generations, a symbol of the powerful force of love and the magic that lay inside the human heart.

"Dear Queen, your kindness has touched so many people; how should we pay you back? asked one of her warriors.

"I don't want anything; instead, just the well-being of my people; that's all that matters—blessings from the divine and heaven," said Princess Chenoa. She was already named Queen Chenoa of Ankaa, the magical land of hope. Those words were conveyed to the rest of the world. People listened to it.

One night, with the blooming moonlight, it was gracefully shining. Her husband, King Noah, was looking at her, and Queen Chenoa was smiling. For him, she was beautiful, like the moonlight. King Noah asked, "Dear Queen, why don't you ask anything after all these years?"

Queen Chenoa smiled again with her teary eyes, looking at the moon and the stars. She was pausing for a few seconds before looking at it.

King Noah asked again. "My Queen?"

Queen Chenoa then answered her king. "Maybe the only thing I asked for is that I want this world to spread kindness to each other. Those things will help so many people in this world. Imagine everything being blessed with goodness, happiness, and kindness instead of sadness, evilness, and hatred toward each other. Right, my king? Maybe someday people will embrace the idea that goodness always wins no matter what by walking the true path.

King Noah finally understood Queen Chenoa's wishes for herself, her people, and the world. King Noah smiled and hugged her. "Actually, my beloved Queen, I have this secret from the day one we met," King Noah said to her.

"What is it?" Queen Chenoa asked.

"Do you remember? That was your first question to me, but I walked away without answers," he answered, leaving her in wonder.

"What do you mean, my beloved King?" she asked again.

"I was actually the Prince of Ankaa; I was always watching you from the far-awakened land of magical hope. I was being chained for a long time ago after the disappearance of Ankaa and my parents were killed by Athena. I was waiting for you until my chain to be broken and until your kindness to touch the world. After all those years, my chain was finally broken. I was also building my own kingdom, my dear. I was the mask man—the one you danced with during your best friend's tying knots.

Queen Chenoa was shocked and exhaled. "It was you, my dear King."

"How miraculous were our destiny?" she then accepted their fate. She hugged again and said, "Now you are free, from the chain of evilness, from the withering land of hope; it's now our magical land of hope,

Ankaa. Let's protect this together, my King, with goodness in it. Together, we united this world full of peace; may we make the world a better place. May the blossoms of kindness flourish in your heart, shining the world with their beauty." She expressed her feelings and wishes.

After that, they watched the moon and the shining stars. There was a beautiful sound from the night sky; they understood that they were being blessed. They were dancing together peacefully.

Thus, Queen Chenoa 's celestial dance, doing kindness and healing, spreading love and giving hope, trust, peace and harmony. They all had culminated in a joyous unity that transcended above kingdoms and surpassed time and space. In the embrace of love, kindness, and unity, they lived happily ever later, their divine adventure an immortal testament of the eternal dance of the heart. That's the journey of Princess Chenoa from a dragon creature turning back into a human being named Queen Chenoa, the Queen of the magical land of hope. Ankaa.

The End

About the Author

"Allwyn Rise is a passionate storyteller whose heart beats to the rhythm of fantasy, romance, adventure, and the enchanting world of magic. With an unwavering love for mythical creatures like dragons and a knack for crafting captivating children's tales, Allwyn transports readers to realms where the extraordinary becomes a part of everyday life. Every word penned by Allwyn is a portal to a world where dreams take flight and love knows no bounds. Prepare to be spellbound as you embark on a journey through Allwyn Rise's magical realms."

Read more at https://www.buymeacoffee.com/eurekatales.